For Julia, my companion on the journey through Sleepy Hollow.—R.V.N.

Copyright © 1989 Rabbit Ears Productions. Inc., Westport, Connecticut.
Rabbit Ears Books is an imprint of Rabbit Ears Productions.
Published by Picture Book Studio Ltd., Saxonville, Massachusetts.
Distributed in Canada by Vanwell Publishing, St. Catharines, Ont.
All rights reserved.
Printed in Hong Kong.
10 9 8 7 6 5 4 3 2 1

Library of Congress Cataloging in Publication Data
Van Nutt, Robert.
The legend of Sleepy Hollow / Washington Irving; adapted by Robert
Van Nutt; illustrated by Robert Van Nutt.
Summary: A superstitious schoolmaster, in love with a wealthy
farmer's daughter, has a terrifying encounter with a headless
horseman.
ISBN 0-88708-088-X
ISBN 0-88708-089-8 (bk & cassette pkg)
[1. Ghosts—Fiction. 2. New York (State)—Fiction.] I. Irving,
Washington, 1783–1859. Legend of Sleepy Hollow. II. Title.
PZ7.V34Le 1989
[Fic]—dc19   88-33375

written by Washington Irving

# THE LEGEND OF
# SLEEPY HOLLOW

adapted and illustrated by Robert Van Nutt

Rabbit Ears Books

Do you believe in ghosts? Well, there are some places where people do—and for good reason!

If you travel up the Hudson River from noisy and crowded New York City, you will come to a cozy little valley, hidden away among high hills where time seems to have stopped. The people who live here are the families of the first Dutch settlers. They like their old ways and see no reason to change or to leave their quiet farmland to travel to the big cities of the outside world. I have heard it said that long before the first white man came, an old Indian chief cast a magic spell on the land. Whether it is true or not, there certainly is an enchanted feeling that hangs over this region and it's easy to believe that some very strange things can happen here. In fact, everything is so dream-like in this little valley that it's known by the name of Sleepy Hollow.

One day, a long time ago, a stranger came to Sleepy Hollow. He was so tall and so thin that you might have mistaken him for some scarecrow that had run away from its cornfield. His name was Ichabod Crane, and he had traveled all the way from Connecticut to be Sleepy Hollow's new schoolteacher.

The schoolhouse was a little one-room building, made of logs. Through its patched windows you could hear the murmur of the students' voices, reading out their lessons, and then…"Whack!"…the frightful sound of the birch rod as it met the bottom of some particularly naughty child.

"It may hurt now," Ichabod Crane would tell the smarting urchin, "but you will remember this lesson and thank me for it for the rest of your days."

You see, he wasn't a cruel man, he just believed in the old motto, "Spare the rod and spoil the child." Ichabod Crane's students were certainly not spoiled…nor were they abused. Indeed, it was wise of him to stay on good terms with his pupils, for he relied on the generosity of their parents for his living.

When school hours were over, he would usually walk some of the smaller children home… especially those who had pretty sisters, or good cooks for mothers. His visits always caused some commotion at a farmhouse.

"Set out the best plates and use the silver teapot," the mothers would instruct their daughters. "Master Crane is a learned gentleman-like person, and I am sure he has vastly superior tastes. Be sure to make extra cakes and sweetmeats, for I never saw a man who could eat as much as the schoolmaster."

Ichabod was particularly happy in the company of the country girls. The more bashful country bumpkins would hang back sheepishly, secretly envying Ichabod's education and the elegant manners he displayed to the ladies.

On cold autumn evenings, Ichabod loved to visit with the old Dutch wives, as they sat spinning by the fire, telling their tales of haunted houses and haunted fields and haunted brooks and haunted bridges, not to mention numerous ghosts and goblins.

It was on one such evening that he first heard the story of the most famous spirit of them all. It was, they said, the ghost of a Hessian trooper who, during the Revolutionary War, had his head shot off by a cannonball!

"They buried his body in the churchyard," said one old dame.

"But they never found his head," added another.

"His ghost rides out in the gloom of the night to the old battlefield where he searches for his lost head."

"And then he thunders back along the roads as if on the wings of the wind until he reaches the church bridge, where he vanishes in a flash of fire and brimstone!"

"He is known as the Headless Horseman of the Hollow."

"Heaven preserve us!" exclaimed Ichabod, who had a most fearful walk home that evening, imagining he saw the ghostly form of the Headless Horseman in every shadow that crossed his path.

Be that as it may, the morning sun sent any ghost or goblin scampering back to its secret lair, and shone once again on the rich and friendly farmland of the Hollow.

On this day, Ichabod found himself summoned to the largest and most prosperous of the Dutch homesteads. It was owned by one Baltus Van Tassel.

"My greatest treasure," boasted old Van Tassel, "is not my full barn, nor my fields of rye, buckwheat, or Indian corn, nor my cattle, nor horses, nor pigs, nor fowls, nor even my house and all the goods therein. No, Sir, my greatest treasure is my daughter and only child, Katrina."

And there she was, Katrina Van Tassel, famed not only for her great beauty, but also for the fact that she stood to inherit all of the Van Tassel wealth.

"Master Crane, Father and I would have you give me lessons in the art of singing," Katrina informed the delighted Ichabod.

He gazed around him in awestruck wonder. His mouth watered as his ever-hungry mind pictured all the bounty of the farm, cooked and ready for the dinner table. And then there was Katrina, rosy-cheeked as one of her Father's peaches, the crowning jewel in this sumptuous setting.

"My peace of mind is at an end!" thought Ichabod. "I must, somehow, by hook or by crook, win the hand of Katrina Van Tassel!"

Now, Ichabod Crane wasn't the only bachelor with his eye on Katrina. Oh, no, there was also Brom Bones. He was the local hero, famed for his great skill in horsemanship and feats of strength and daring. When any madcap prank took place, the neighbors always smiled, shook their heads and said, "Brom Bones must be at the bottom of it." This hero had singled out Katrina as the object of his gallantries, and though he had courted her for some time, Brom had never actually asked her for her hand in marriage. It was whispered that Katrina would have gladly accepted Brom's offer. Well, that was the situation Ichabod had to contend with. Considering all things, a stronger man would have shrunk from the competition. A wiser man would have despaired.

Ichabod made his advances in a quiet and subtle way. Using the excuse of giving singing lessons, he made frequent visits to the manor house. And so, while the busy dame Van Tassel worked at her spinning wheel, and the honest Balt sat smoking his evening pipe, Ichabod would pay court to Katrina.

"The devil take that schoolmaster!" fumed Brom Bones. "Every time I visit the Van Tassels, Ichabod Crane is there—singing with Katrina! I'll double that schoolmaster up, and stick him on a shelf in his own schoolhouse!"

Ichabod was too conscious of the superior might of Bones to give him any such opportunity. As a result, Ichabod became the object of practical jokes played by Brom and his gang of Sleepy Hollow boys. Things went on this way for some time without Brom being able to discourage the elusive Ichabod.

One fine autumn afternoon, as Ichabod sat watching over his schoolroom, a messenger came clattering up to the door.

"Master Crane, you are hereby invited to attend the merrymaking-quilting frolic to be held this very evening at the home of the Van Tassels."

All was now hustle and hubbub. Books were flung aside and the whole school was turned out an hour early. The gallant Ichabod spent at least an extra half-hour arranging his locks and brushing his best and only suit. He borrowed a horse from an old Dutch farmer, so that he might make his appearance before Katrina in the true style of a romantic cavalier. The animal, named Gunpowder, was a broken-down plough horse that had outlived everything but his bad temper. Thus, gallantly mounted, Ichabod rode forth like a knight of old in search of adventure.

It was towards evening that Ichabod arrived at the Van Tassel manor. He found it thronged with the local people, all turned out in their best attire. Brom Bones was there, as usual the hero of the scene. He had come to the gathering on his favorite horse, Daredevil, a creature like himself, full of mettle and mischief.

Oh! The world of charms that burst upon the ever-hungry Ichabod as he entered the Van Tassel's mansion.

"Welcome, Master Crane," greeted Katrina. "I'm so pleased you could come. Won't you have something to eat? There are doughnuts and Oly Koek and crullers: sweet-cakes and short-cakes, ginger-cakes and honey-cakes. And there's apple pie, peach pie and pumpkin pie. There's ham and smoked beef, and here preserved plums, and peaches and pears, and quinces. And here are boiled shad and roasted chickens. I know, I'll just give you some of each!"

And she did.

Ichabod's eyes rolled with delight as he ate.

"To think, soon I might be master of all this luxury and splendor!"

And now the sound of music summoned all to the dance. The fiddler's bow worked its magic on Ichabod, enlivening every inch of his delighted frame. How could our flogger of urchins be anything but animated and joyous? The lady of his heart was smiling graciously in reply to all his amorous oglings. All the while, the frustrated Brom Bones, sorely smitten with love and jealousy, sat brooding by himself in a corner.

When the dancing was over, Ichabod joined a group of elders who sat out on the porch, smoking their long clay pipes and telling their wild and wonderful legends. They told of the Woman in White who haunted the dark glen at Raven Rock.

"She was on her way home one night when a sudden snowstorm caught her out in the open. She took shelter in a cleft in the rock, but it did her no good, she froze to death before dawn. And to this day, you can still hear her bone-chilling shrieks on cold winter nights, just before a storm."

The old folks all puffed on their pipes and nodded their heads in agreement.

Now Brom Bones spoke up.

"A fearful thing happend to Hans Van Ripper last night. He was chased all along the church road by none other than the ghost of the Headless Horseman! Yes, and poor old Van Ripper was nearly carried off to hell by the goblin. He would have been, too, but he reached the church bridge first, beating out the headless ghost, who, all of a sudden, vanished in a flash of fire."

His listeners all shook their heads, muttering, "Lucky old Hans."

The party now began to break up.
The old farmers gathered their
families in their wagons, and were
heard for some time, rattling along the
roads and over the distant hills. Ichabod was
the last to leave, and in the very witching
time of night, he mounted old Gunpowder
and set out for home.

All the tales of ghosts and goblins that he
had heard that evening now suddenly came
back to him. The night grew darker and
darker. The road now led into the very
shadow of Raven Rock. As he approached
this terrible spot, Ichabod cast frightened
glances to the right and to the left for any
sign of the ghostly Woman in White.
Suddenly he heard a groan—his teeth
chattered at the sound; but it was only one
tree branch rubbing on another as they
swayed in the breeze. He passed in safety,
but new dangers lay ahead.

A small brook crossed the road and ran into a dark hollow called Wiley's Swamp. A few rough logs served as a bridge over this stream. Ichabod attempted to dash quickly across the bridge, but old Gunpowder came to a short stop and refused to move. In the dark shadow of the grove, Ichabod saw something huge and misshapen.

His heart began to thump as he demanded, "Who are you?"

There was no reply.

Once again he called out, "Who are you? Speak!" Ichabod's hair stood on end as the silence continued.

The schoolmaster used both whip and heel on old Gunpowder, who finally started forward. But the shadowy figure was also in motion. Ichabod urged Gunpowder to a faster pace. But the stranger quickened his horse to equal it. As they came to the top of a hill, the dark figure could be seen clearly against the sky. The stranger was headless!— not only that, he carried his severed head in front of him on the saddle!

Ichabod's terror rose to desperation. He showered kicks and blows on the terrified Gunpowder, who leapt into action. But the specter started full jump with him. Away they dashed, stones flying, sparks flashing at every bound! Over the road, plunging down, into the Hollow they raced! Over logs, under branches, galloping side by side.

"Faster! Faster!" Ichabod urged.

Gunpowder bolted ahead. Suddenly, his saddle slipped from beneath him. It fell to earth, trampled under the thundering hooves of the demon horse.

Ichabod clung desperately to the neck of old Gunpowder, as he raced for his life. An opening in the trees ahead revealed the church bridge. "If I can reach that bridge, I'm safe."

Another kick in the ribs, and old Gunpowder sprang onto the bridge. He thundered over the planks. He reached the opposite side. Ichabod cast a look behind, hoping to see the ghostly Horseman vanish in a flash of fire and brimstone. Instead, he saw the goblin rising in his stirrups, in the very act of hurling his head at him. Ichabod tried to dodge, but too late! It hit him with a tremendous CRASH!

The next morning, old Gunpowder was found without his saddle, happily chomping the grass at his master's gate. Ichabod did not make his appearance at breakfast. His students assembled at the schoolhouse, but no schoolmaster. In one part of the road leading to the church, the saddle was found, trampled in the dirt. There were tracks of horses' hooves which led to the bridge, where the hat of the unfortunate Ichabod was discovered, and close beside it, most curious, a shattered pumpkin. The brook was searched, but the body of the schoolmaster was never found.

Shortly after the disappearance of Ichabod, all of Sleepy Hollow rejoiced at the wedding of Katrina and Brom. Could it be, as some whispered, that Katrina's encouragement to the schoolmaster was merely a trick to get Brom to the altar? As to Brom Bones, some suspected that he knew more than he chose to tell about the disappearance of Ichabod, for whenever the story was told, he always burst into a hearty laugh—especially at the mention of the pumpkin.

It is true that Hans Van Ripper, who had been down to New York on a visit several years after, brought home news that Master Crane was still alive and married to a plump and wealthy widow, who just happened to own a prosperous tavern, famed for its good food. But of course, we only have old Hans' word on that. The old country wives, however, who are the best judges of these matters, maintain that Ichabod was spirited away by supernatural means.

To this day, the local people swear that on crisp autumn evenings, in the road by the church bridge, you can still hear the echo of hoofbeats and see, rushing by, like mist blown by the wind, the ghosts of Ichabod Crane and the Headless Horseman of Sleepy Hollow.